THIS BOOK BELONGS TO

Betsy

Jenny
Learns a Lesson

GYO FUJIKAWA

GROSSET & DUNLAP · PUBLISHERS · NEW YORK

A FILMWAYS COMPANY

Jenny is a little girl who likes to play pretend.

One day she had a great idea.

She went to her playhouse where she kept all sorts of clothes and things. She dressed herself up. Then she called her friends to come over.

Sam and Mei Su and Nicholas and
Shags the dog came running.
  "Let's pretend," Jenny said.
  "Pretend what?" Nicholas asked.
  "Pretend I'm a queen,"
Jenny said.

  "What does that mean?"
asked Mei Su.
  "I wear a crown and a robe, and
I carry a royal stick," Jenny answered.
  "And what do WE do?" Sam asked.

"You do what I tell you to,"
Jenny said. "A queen tells
everybody what to do."

"And they do it?" Nicholas asked.
"Of course, silly!" Jenny said.
"No one would think of not
doing what the queen says. . . .

Now, Mei Su, you hold my robe.
Nicholas, you and Sam are soldiers.
You follow behind Mei Su. Shags, you
are the royal watchdog. Come along—
we're off to the palace!"

At first Sam and Nicholas and Mei Su and Shags did what Jenny told them to. But after a while they stopped and walked away.

"Come back," Jenny shouted. "I'm the queen! You have to do what I say!"

"We don't like queens," Mei Su said.

"Or kings, neither," Nicholas added.

"Even pretend ones," Sam said.

And Shags growled.

The next day Jenny had another
pretend idea.
She dressed up in dancing clothes and
put flowers in her hair. Then she asked
Mei Su and Nicholas and Sam and Shags over.

"This time," Jenny told them, "I'm a famous
dancer, and I teach people how to dance."

Mei Su and Nicholas and Sam
all thought that dancing
would be great fun.

Mei Su did a little
dance she made up herself.

Sam picked up a cane and
pretended he was a tap dancer.

And Nicholas leaped high in the air,
then did a somersault and stood on his hands.

Sam and Nicholas and Mei Su—and
even Shags—were so interested in their
own dancing, they didn't pay any attention
to Jenny.

This made Jenny angry. "No, no, no!"
she cried. "You must do MY kind of
dancing. I'm the best dancer in the world.
Follow me!"

But Sam and Nicholas and Mei Su and Shags kept on dancing the way they each wanted to.

And this made Jenny so angry, she went home and shut the door.

The following afternoon, Jenny wasn't angry anymore. When she got together with Sam and Nicholas and Mei Su and Shags, she said,

"Today we are going to have a wonderful time. We'll play pirate. I have pirate clothes for all of you, and I'll be Captain Jenny."

When everybody was dressed up, Jenny said,
"Now come along. We're on our way to find buried
treasure. You, Sam, carry my boat to the pond.
And Nicholas, bring along my pirate flag. Mei Su,
say, 'Yo-ho! Yo-ho!' And Shags, look fierce and bark."

After they reached the pond, Jenny got in the boat
and ordered her friends to push it out into the water.

Sam and Nicholas and Mei Su and Shags waited on
shore while Jenny floated to the middle of the pond.
Suddenly Jenny shouted, "Help! Help! Rescue me!"
"Rescue yourself!" Nicholas said.
"You know what to do about everything," Sam said.
"We're staying right here," Mei Su said.
"You can't treat your pirate captain this way!"
Jenny yelled.

"Let's go home," Mei Su said.
"It's no fun playing pirates."
"Suits me," Sam said.
"Me, too," Nicholas said.
And Shags growled.
They all went away,
        leaving Jenny yelling.

   After a while Jenny gave up, and she
waded ashore.
   "I must think of something we can play
together," she said to herself.

The next day, Jenny had another idea.
She asked Sam and Nicholas and Mei Su
and Shags over to the playhouse. When they
arrived, she was all dressed up in her very
best finery.

"I'm a grand duchess," she told them.
"And I'm inviting you to tea."

"What's a duchess?" Sam asked.

"A great lady," Jenny said. "It's an honor to have tea with me."

"Is it?" Nicholas asked.

"Yes, and how charmed I am to have you visit me," Jenny answered very grandly. "But first, before we have tea, you must go and wash your hands and faces."

Sam and Nicholas and Mei Su and Shags were tired of being told what to do.

So they left the grand duchess to have tea all by herself.

When the friends had gone a short distance,
they sat down and began talking:

"Jenny's too bossy!"
"Jenny wants everybody to do what she says!"
"Jenny thinks she's so smart!"
And Shags growled.
Sam and Nicholas and Mei Su and Shags stayed
away from Jenny for several days.

As for Jenny, she missed
her friends. She wasn't happy.
She began to think about why
they didn't have fun anymore.

She thought
about it
day and night.

One morning Jenny woke up and she had a
marvelous idea. It was the best idea ever!

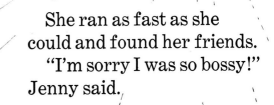

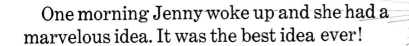

She ran as fast as she
could and found her friends.
"I'm sorry I was so bossy!"
Jenny said.

"I'm sorry I tried to make everybody do what
I said. I wasn't nice at all. Please forgive me!"
"Of course, we forgive you," Mei Su said.
"We sure do," Sam said.
"That goes for me, too," Nicholas said.
Shags jumped up and down and wagged his tail.

The friends were all happy to be together again.
"Let's all go to the playhouse and really have
a good time!" Jenny said.

And they all did. Sam and Nicholas and Mei Su
and Shags and Jenny dressed up in all sorts of things,
and pretended to be whatever they wanted to be.

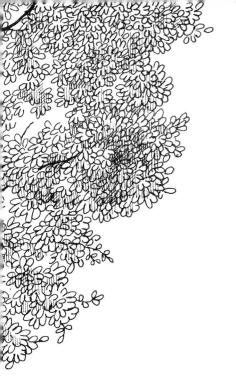

They had a wonderful day. After a while
Sam said, "I'm tired."

"I'm sleepy," Mei Su yawned.

"My eyes are closing," Jenny said softly.

"Mine, too," Nicholas whispered.

Shags didn't say anything.

He was already fast asleep.